Disney
Sleeping Beauty

Ladybird

Once upon a time, in a faraway land, there lived a king called Stefan and his beautiful queen. For years they had longed for a child, and when at last a lovely baby daughter was born to them, the whole kingdom rejoiced.

The King declared that the new Princess would be called Aurora because, like the dawn, she had brought sunlight into their lives. A holiday was proclaimed to celebrate her birth.

On the day of the celebration, trumpeters played fanfares and bells rang out in every corner of the land. Crowds of people arrived at the palace, wearing their finest clothes and bringing gifts for the baby Princess.

One of the guests was King Hubert, the ruler of a nearby kingdom, who arrived with his son, Prince Philip. The two Kings smiled as the little Prince looked into the cradle at the baby Princess.

"For years we have dreamed that our kingdoms would unite, Hubert," said King Stefan. "At last it will be possible."

"We will announce the betrothal of my son to your daughter this very day," said King Hubert.

"When they grow up they will be married, and the two kingdoms will become one," agreed King Stefan. "Oh, this is indeed a special day, my old friend!"

Just then, a brilliant light filled the room and in floated three good fairies, Flora, Fauna and Merryweather. They each had a gift for Princess Aurora.

Flora, the fairy in red, went first. "My gift shall be the gift of beauty," she said, waving her wand. A mass of tiny flowers fell into the cradle, vanishing as they touched the coverlet.

Fauna was next, wearing green, her favourite colour.

"Tiny Princess, my gift shall be the gift of song," she said.

Little songbirds flew around the room, trilling sweetly.

Finally it was time for the
fairy in blue, Merryweather, to
step forward.

Lifting her wand, she began,
"Sweet Princess, my gift shall be…"

Suddenly the doors flew open, banging against the walls. A great gust of wind howled through the room, and thunder and lightning ripped the air.

A flame flared up in the middle of the hall, and a terrible figure, carrying a raven, stepped out of it.

"It's Maleficent, the evil fairy!" gasped Fauna.

"*Why was I not invited?*" asked Maleficent, in a voice as cold as ice.

The King knew that this wicked fairy had caused much harm in his kingdom, and he thought carefully before he replied.

"It must have been an oversight," he said at last. "We hope you are not offended."

Maleficent's eyes narrowed.

"Of course not," she said. "And to show I bear no ill will, I too have a gift to bestow on the baby."

She turned to the cradle.

18

"The Princess shall indeed grow in grace and beauty, beloved by all who know her," Maleficent began. "But before the sun sets on her sixteenth birthday, she shall prick her finger on the spindle of a spinning wheel – *and die!*"

"Oh no!" cried the Queen. She snatched up the baby and held her tightly.

King Stefan ordered the guards to seize Maleficent, but before they could reach her, the evil fairy vanished in flames. Only the echo of her horrible laughter lingered in the air.

Merryweather broke the stunned silence. "I still have my gift to bestow," she said. "I cannot undo the evil spell, for Maleficent's powers are far too great. But I can soften it."

The fairy raised her wand and said,

"Sweet Princess,
If through this wicked witch's trick
A spindle should your finger prick,
A ray of hope there still may be
In this the gift I give to thee.
Not in death, but just in sleep
The fateful prophecy you'll keep,
And from this slumber you shall wake
When true love's kiss the spell shall break."

"So Her Royal Highness will not die from pricking her finger, after all?" asked King Stefan.

"That's right," replied Fauna. "Merryweather's spell means that she will fall asleep instead, until awakened by the kiss of true love."

"That's good," said the King. "All the same, it would be better if she couldn't prick her finger at all. Every spinning wheel in the land must be burned!"

Messengers sped through the kingdom, telling people to burn their spinning wheels. Soon, the King was sure that every single one had been destroyed.

The three good fairies were still uneasy about the wicked spell.

"I'm sure it will all work out," said Fauna uncertainly. "Let's all have a nice cup of tea."

"Burning spindles won't stop Maleficent," said Merryweather. "I'd like to turn her into a toad!"

"You know our magic can only be used for good," said Flora. "Now listen – I've had an idea. We could take Aurora to live with us in the forest, and keep her safe until Maleficent's curse has passed!"

"You mean – *we* would look after the *baby*?" asked Fauna.

"Why not?" said Merryweather. "We'd have our magic to help us."

"No!" said Flora. "No magic. No wands. No wings. If we used those, Maleficent would find us – and Aurora. We must transform ourselves into peasant women!"

The hardest part of Flora's plan was convincing the King and Queen that they must part with the Princess for sixteen years. The royal couple were very unhappy, but they knew that Aurora's safety was more important than anything.

The King and Queen kissed their baby daughter goodbye. They watched sadly from a balcony, as the three good fairies later carried the little Princess away into the forest, under cover of darkness.

The fairies found a deserted cottage deep in the forest. It was small, but warm and snug inside.

"This is a poor dwelling for a princess," said Merryweather.

"Hush!" said Flora. "You must never use the word princess again! From now on, we must pretend that she is our little niece. We mustn't even use her real name, in case Maleficent hears about it."

"What shall we call her, then?" asked Fauna.

"Let's call her Briar Rose," said Flora.

So from that day on they called the Princess by her new name, and they gave her all the love and care they could.

Without their magic to help them, the fairies had to do all the cooking, washing and cleaning, themselves.

As the years passed, the little baby grew into a beautiful, young girl. She was as pretty as a wild rose, and she was always happy. Briar Rose did not know that she was really a princess.

The fairies were happy too – except when they thought about the future.

One day the fairies were watching the Princess through the cottage window. "Soon she will be sixteen," sighed Fauna sadly, "and we shall have to give her back. But we have had her to ourselves for nearly sixteen years. Her parents will be overjoyed to see her again. We must not be selfish."

Maleficent was also thinking of the future. For nearly sixteen years she had hunted for the Princess, without success.

Her soldiers always returned empty-handed.

"Have you searched in *every* corner of the land?" asked Maleficent, finally.

"Yes – in all the mountains, and all the valleys – and in all the cradles," said the captain.

"*Fools!*" screeched their evil mistress. "Have you been looking for a baby all these years? *Idiots! Imbeciles! She is a baby no longer!*"

Maleficent turned to her raven. Lovingly she stroked its feathers.

"Go!" she cried. "Search for a maid of sixteen with hair of sunshine gold, and lips red as the rose. Do not fail me!"

The raven flew off at once.

The evil fairy watched
until it became a speck too
small to see, swooping over
the distant hills.

She knew that the sharp-eyed
bird would search tirelessly.
If anyone could find Aurora,
it would be the raven.

On the morning of Briar Rose's sixteenth birthday, the
three fairies were planning lots of delightful surprises for her.
But they could do nothing while Briar Rose was there.

"Go out and pick some wild berries, dear," said Flora.

"But we've still got the ones I picked yesterday," said Briar Rose.

"We need some more," said Flora firmly. "Off you go!"

"And don't speak to any strangers on the way!" called Merryweather.

As soon as Briar Rose was out of sight, Fauna began to make a birthday cake. It was going to have fifteen layers, with flowers and candles on top.

Briar Rose sang as she walked along, picking berries. She loved living in the forest, because she had so many friends there. She loved all the creatures who made their homes in the trees and played in the mossy banks, and they loved her.

Birds flew down to greet her. Rabbits hopped along at her feet, and a squirrel woke from his daytime nap to listen to her sweet song.

Nearby, a handsome young man was riding through the forest.

"Can you hear that beautiful voice, Samson?" he asked his horse. "Let's see if we can find its owner."

Briar Rose had begun to dance to the tune of her song, and she didn't hear the young man approaching. He slipped from the horse's back and stood behind her, gently taking her wrists in his hands.

"Oh!" gasped Briar Rose.

"I'm awfully sorry," said the young man. "I didn't mean to frighten you." He let go of her wrists, and Briar Rose turned round.

"I'm not frightened," said Briar Rose, looking up at him. "It's just that you're a… stranger."

"But I'm sure we've met before," said the young man, "once upon a dream…"

And they began to dance, while the birds and animals looked on.

Suddenly Briar Rose remembered the berries, and her aunts.

"I must go!" she cried, breaking away from the young man.

"Wait!" he pleaded. "I don't even know your name! When can I see you again?"

"This evening – at the cottage in the glen," replied Briar Rose.

Then she ran away.

Back at the cottage, the fairies were in a dreadful muddle.

Flora and Merryweather had tried to make a special gown for Briar Rose, but neither of them could sew very well.

Fauna had done her best with the birthday cake, but for some reason it wouldn't stand up.

"Oh dear!" cried Merryweather. "Briar Rose will be back in a minute, and everything is in such a mess!"

"It's no good," said Flora at last. "We'll have to use our wands... just this once!"

Merryweather ran to the cupboard where they had hidden the wands so long ago. Flora waved hers at the dress...

…and Fauna waved hers at the cake.

"That's better!" they all said together.

Then they waved the wands around the cottage, until everything was sparkling, clean and tidy again.

The magic sparks from the wands flew up out of the cottage chimney.

As luck would have it, at that very moment Maleficent's evil raven was flying through the forest.

He saw the sparks and swooped down to find out what was going on.

"That's magic," he croaked. "And what is magic doing in a woodland cottage, I'd like to know?"

He flew off to tell Maleficent!

Briar Rose arrived back at the cottage with a happy heart.

"Oh, thank you all!" she exclaimed. "What a beautiful dress! And such a lovely cake!

"This is the happiest day of my life. I'm in love!" she sighed.

She told her aunts all about the young man she had met in the forest.

"Why aren't you happy for me?" she asked, when she saw the worried looks on their faces.

"I'm afraid – you're betrothed already, dear," said Fauna. "To Prince Philip."

"But that's impossible," said Briar Rose. "How could I marry a prince?"

"Because you're really the Princess Aurora," said Flora. "And we're taking you back to your royal parents tonight."

"But he's coming here this evening!" cried Briar Rose.

"We're sorry, dear," said Flora. "But you are the Princess Aurora now, and you must never see that young man again."

It was a sad group that set off for the palace. Princess Aurora was thinking of her young man, and the fairies were thinking of how soon they would lose her. They were sad, too, because they knew she was unhappy.

At the palace, King Stefan and King Hubert were raising their goblets in a toast.

"Here's to the happy couple!" said King Stefan.

"And to a rosy future!" agreed King Hubert.

In another part of the palace, the fairies left Princess Aurora alone to wait for her parents. When she grew tired of sitting in one place, she began to explore. There was a door…

She peeped round it and saw a tall woman dressed in black.

"Come in, my dear," said Maleficent silkily. "I have a present for you – a spinning wheel!"

Aurora moved towards it, but voices in her ear made her hesitate.

"*Don't touch anything!*" said the voices.

"Touch it!" said Maleficent.

"*Anything, anything!*" said the voices.

"Touch it, I say!" said Maleficent.

Aurora put out her hand…

She caught her finger on the spindle, which pricked her sharply. With a gasp, she fell to the floor.

Maleficent cackled horribly.

"Now to find the Prince!" she said. "He must not save her with the kiss of love!"

It was the three good fairies who found Aurora. They knew at once what had happened, and they were horrified.

"Poor King Stefan – and the Queen!" said Fauna.

"Yes," said Merryweather. "They'll be heartbroken when they find that the prophecy has come true."

"They're not going to find out," said Flora. "We'll put them all to sleep. They'll awaken only when the Princess does."

So, as the sun was setting, the three fairies flitted through the palace, sprinkling sleeping dust over everyone.

Just as King Hubert was dropping off, the fairies heard him telling King Stefan, "Philip… he's fallen in love… with a peasant girl… met her in the forest this morning…"

The fairies looked at one another.

"Oh!" exclaimed Flora. "That must mean… Briar Rose's young man is…"

"Prince Philip!" chorused the other two.

63

"Come on!" said Flora. "We've got to get back to the cottage!"

The three fairies headed back to the forest, flying as fast as they could.

"I do hope we get there in time," said Fauna. "Maleficent will be looking for him, too. We *must* find him before she does!"

But it was too late. Even as Fauna spoke, Prince Philip
was hurrying towards the cottage in the glen. He was eager to
see the girl he loved.

As he knocked on the door, he could hear someone moving
about inside.

"Good – she is at home," he thought.

The door swung open. But instead of the lovely girl he expected, there stood a group of strange creatures. They leapt upon him and began tying him up before he could fight them off.

Maleficent smiled as she watched her soldiers do her bidding.

"Take him to my castle," she ordered, when they had finished. "I have plans for my royal guest!"

In the deepest, darkest dungeon of Maleficent's castle, Philip struggled against his chains.

Maleficent stood at the top of the steps and gloated.

"Why are you doing this?" cried Philip.

"Oh, why so melancholy, Prince Philip?" replied Maleficent. "Just think of your true love, your peasant girl, who is really the Princess Aurora. She sleeps in her father's castle, dreaming of the prince who will awaken her with a kiss. But will he still be a young man when he regains his freedom? Or will he remain imprisoned until he is an old, old man?"

Smiling evilly, she left.

Prince Philip stared miserably down at the floor. He didn't notice the three tiny fairies who flew in through the bars of the window. But once they were inside, the fairies returned to normal size – and Philip could hardly believe his eyes.

"Who…" he began.

"Ssh!" whispered Flora. "No time to explain!" Using their wands, the fairies broke the chains and the lock on the door.

"You'll face many dangers," said Flora. "Take this Shield of Virtue, and this mighty Sword of Truth. They always triumph over Evil." The sword and shield flew into the Prince's hands.

"Now go to the palace," said Flora. "The Princess is waiting for your kiss!"

Prince Philip wasted no time. He found his horse and rode off at high speed. But Maleficent's raven saw him leave, and it flew to tell its mistress.

When the Prince reached the palace, an enormous hedge of thorns barred his way.

"This is Maleficent's work," he thought, as he hacked at the thorns with the Sword of Truth.

On the bridge that spanned
the palace moat, an evil-smelling
wind made Prince Philip falter.

As he struggled to breathe,
an enormous dragon appeared
in front of him, blocking his way.

"Maleficent!" cried the Prince,
realizing that his enemy had
transformed herself into this
monster. "You will not stop me!"

The dragon drew itself up,
ready to strike, but brave Prince
Philip leapt off his horse and
held high the Sword of Truth.

A cackle of horrible laughter came from the dragon's mouth. It was followed by a torrent of flames and poisonous gas.

Just in time, Philip remembered the Shield of Virtue. As he held it up in front of him, he heard the flames sizzle on its solid surface. Behind it, he was safe.

Enraged, the dragon reared up and charged at the Prince, knocking the shield from his hand. But he still had the Sword of Truth!

Philip drew back his arm and, with all his strength, threw the Sword at the dragon.

The steel glinted as it flew straight and true – right into the dragon's heart. With a mighty crash, Maleficent fell dead.

Prince Philip rushed into the palace. He hardly noticed the sleeping courtiers. He did not even see his own father, asleep next to his friend King Stefan. Philip was looking for the Princess.

He found her at last in an upstairs bedroom, where Flora, Fauna and Merryweather had taken her. Gently, Prince Philip kissed her.

Princess Aurora opened her eyes and recognized her true love.

81

All over the palace, people began to wake up. Flora, Fauna and Merryweather flew round and round, checking that all was well.

It was. They had cast their spell so perfectly that the two kings continued their conversation without realizing that they had been interrupted.

"It's time for the festivities to begin," said King Hubert.

"Quite," said King Stefan. "Where's Aurora?"

"Mother! Father!" cried Aurora.

There she stood, her arms outstretched to greet them.

"Aurora – my darling child!" cried the Queen, running to hug her daughter.

"You are truly beautiful. Just like your mother!" said the overjoyed King Stefan.

When the Prince introduced Aurora to his father, she kissed him on the cheek.

King Hubert chuckled with delight. "This is the best kiss of the day!" he said.

"Oh, I don't know about that," said Prince Philip. He looked at Aurora, and she smiled back, remembering the kiss that had awakened her.

The news spread quickly throughout the land, and people everywhere began to celebrate.

At the palace, a wonderful ball was given in honour of Princess Aurora and Prince Philip, and their wedding day was announced. As the music began, the Prince took Aurora in his arms to lead the dancing.

But no sound could drown the happy chatter of the three fairies, Flora, Fauna and Merryweather. Once more they had become invisible, but they were still there – as they always would be, watching over their beloved Princess.

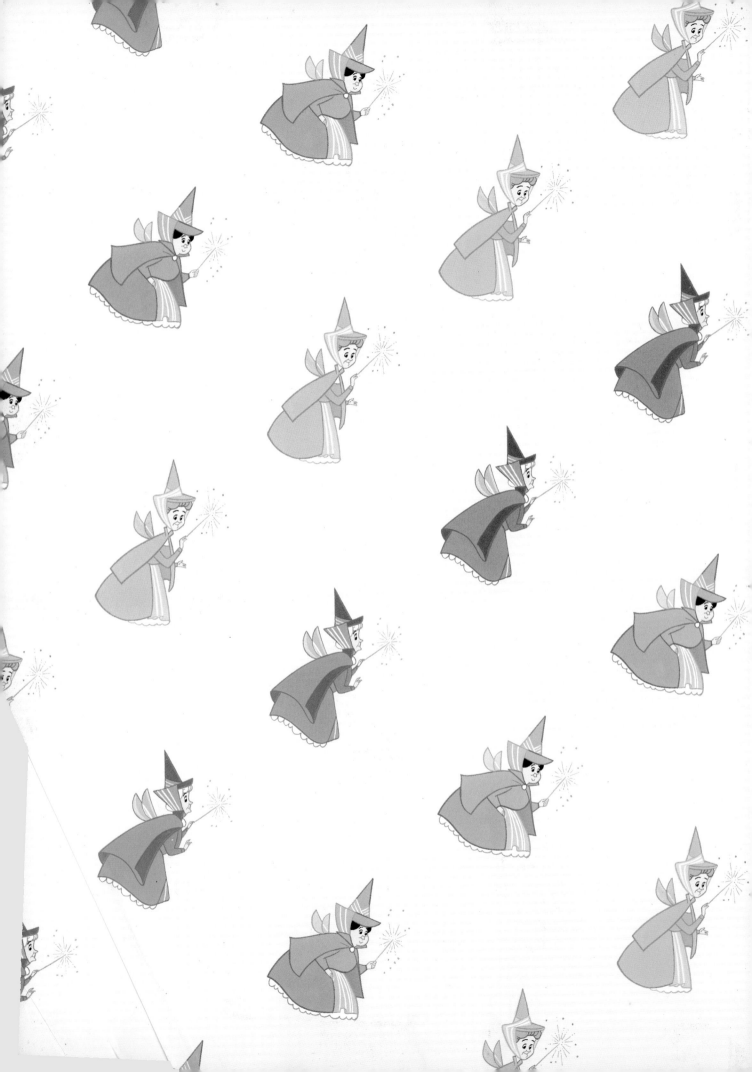